Lunar Fluffies

BBC
CHILDREN'S BOOKS

It was a shivery start to the day in Moona Luna.

A cup of hot cosmic cocoa for space adventurer Lunar Jim and Ripple, the engineer, was the most exciting thing to happen so far today.

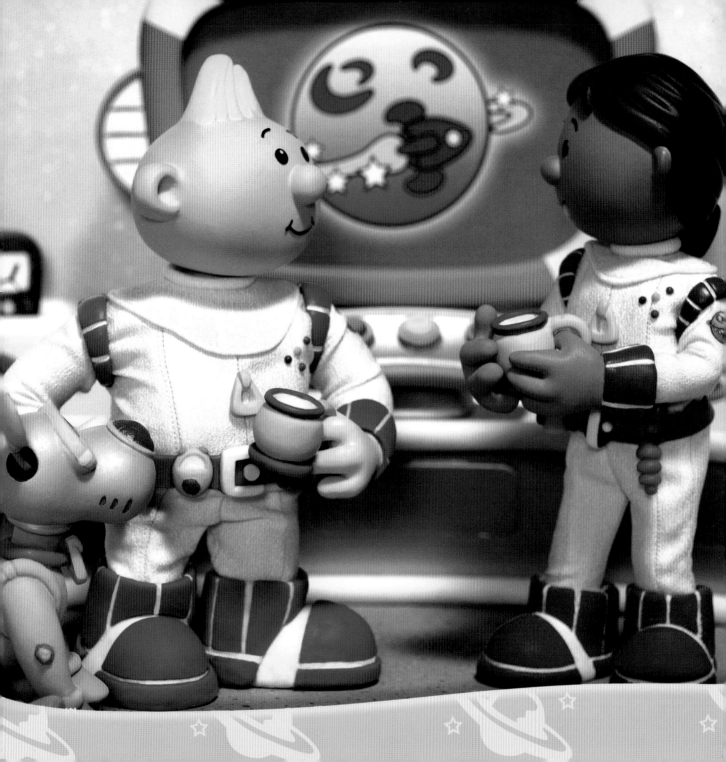

"**Brrr...** it's freezing!" shivered Jim, as Eco appeared on the View Comm.

"Jim, those crystals we collected yesterday give off heat as well as light!" cried Eco excitedly.

"We need more of those crystals right away!" shouted Jim. "Let's get lunar!"

T.E.D. was keen to get warm, so he went with Jim and Rover to find more crystals.

"I happen to be an expert at finding crystals, Jim," shivered T.E.D. "Especially if they are going to keep me warm!"

In the first cave they explored, Rover's bleeps and blips told them he'd found an interesting furry creature.

But T.E.D. insisted, "L-let's g-get to C-crystal C-cave b- before I t-turn into Icicle T-T.E.D.!

Strangely, as they left, the furry creature followed them...

Back at Mission Control, Ripple and Eco were delighted when the lunar explorers brought back plenty of new crystals.

While the others were busy warming themselves, Rover spotted the furry blue creature he'd seen in the cave.

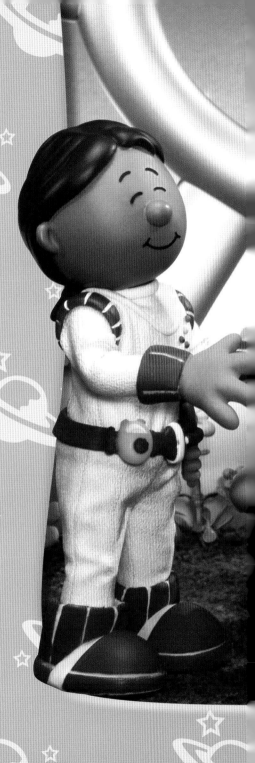

"Ahhh! What's that? Save me!" squealed a terrified T.E.D. "Save my crystal, then save yourselves!"

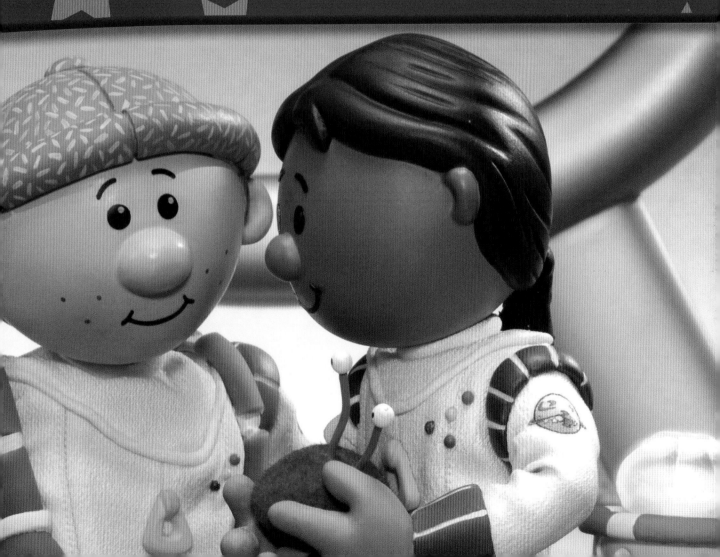

Ripple picked up the cuddly creature with a smile. "I've always wanted a pet," she said, stroking it gently. "I'm going to call it a Fluffy."

Next morning at the Ecodome, there were Fluffies everywhere!

"They must have appeared in the night," said Eco.

Jim was puzzled. "I wonder why the Fluffies came here?"

"It's obviously because they love me!" declared T.E.D., as Fluffies climbed all over him.

"But we don't have space for them here," said Ripple. "We'd better return them to the cave before any more of them turn up."

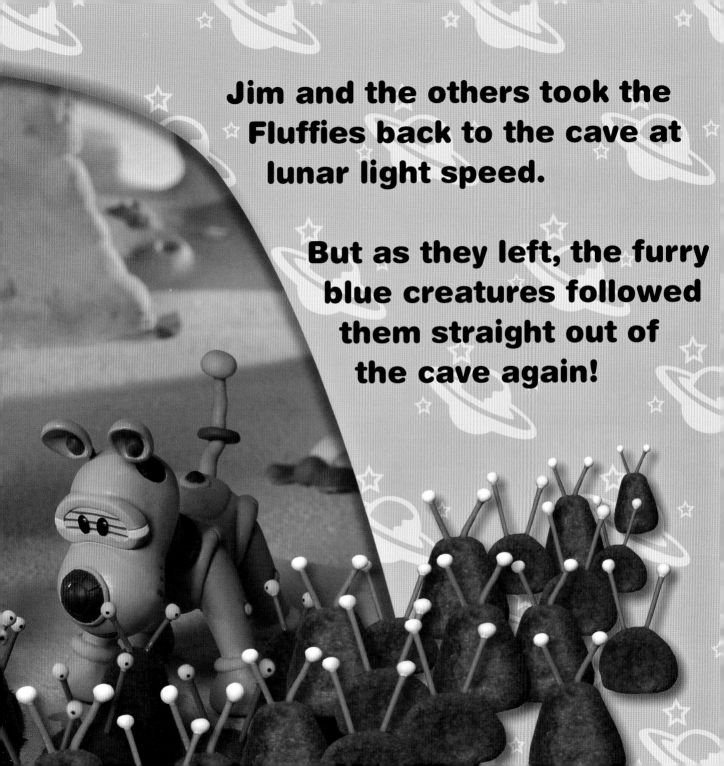

Jim and the others took the Fluffies back to the cave at lunar light speed.

But as they left, the furry blue creatures followed them straight out of the cave again!

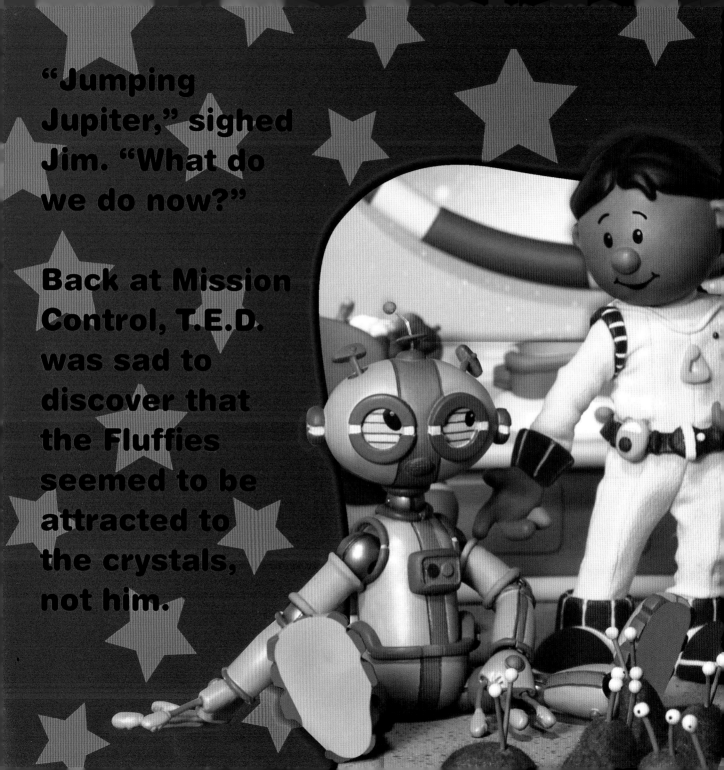

"Jumping Jupiter," sighed Jim. "What do we do now?"

Back at Mission Control, T.E.D. was sad to discover that the Fluffies seemed to be attracted to the crystals, not him.

Suddenly, Jim understood the answer to their puzzle.

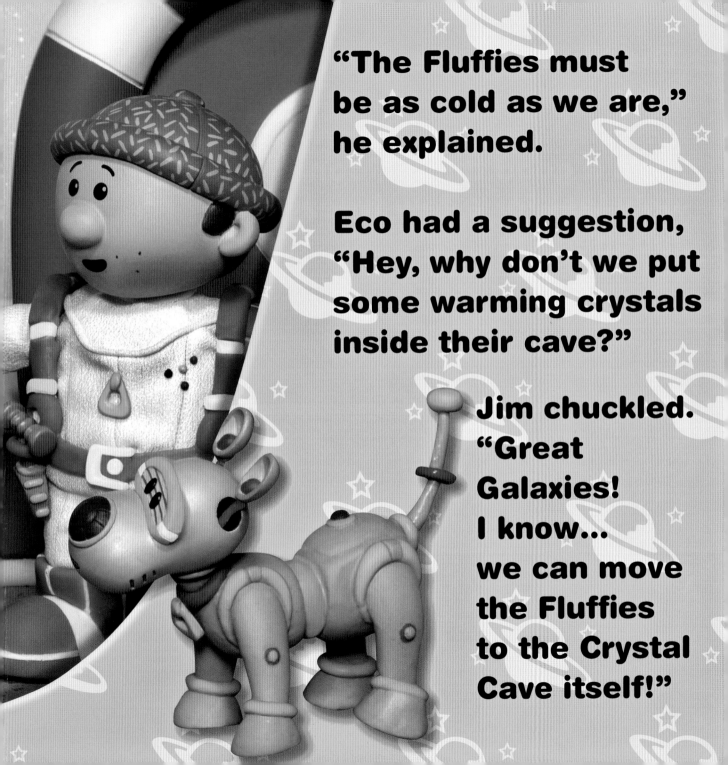

"The Fluffies must be as cold as we are," he explained.

Eco had a suggestion, "Hey, why don't we put some warming crystals inside their cave?"

Jim chuckled. "Great Galaxies! I know... we can move the Fluffies to the Crystal Cave itself!"

The Fluffies were very happy with their new home.

"It's a good thing Moona Luna winters only last for a few freezy days!" laughed Jim.

THE END